ATOMIC!

THE MADNESS OF MADAME MALICE

To my brother Ian,
and to the worlds we made on the weekends

First published in the UK in 2012 by Scholastic Children's Books
An imprint of Scholastic Ltd
Euston House, 24 Eversholt Street
London, NW1 1DB, UK
Registered office: Westfield Road, Southam, Warwickshire, CV47 0RA
SCHOLASTIC and associated logos are trademarks and/
or registered trademarks of Scholastic Inc.

Text copyright © Guy Bass, 2012
Illustrations copyright © Jamie Littler, 2012

The right of Guy Bass and Jamie Littler to be identified as the author
and illustrator of this work has been asserted by them.

Cover illustration © Jamie Littler, 2012

ISBN 978 1407 11123 0

A CIP catalogue record for this book
is available from the British Library.

Printed and bound by CPI Group (UK) Ltd, Croydon, CR0 4YY
Papers used by Scholastic Children's Books are made
from wood grown in sustainable forests.

1 3 5 7 9 10 8 6 4 2

www.scholastic.co.uk/zone
www.guybass.com

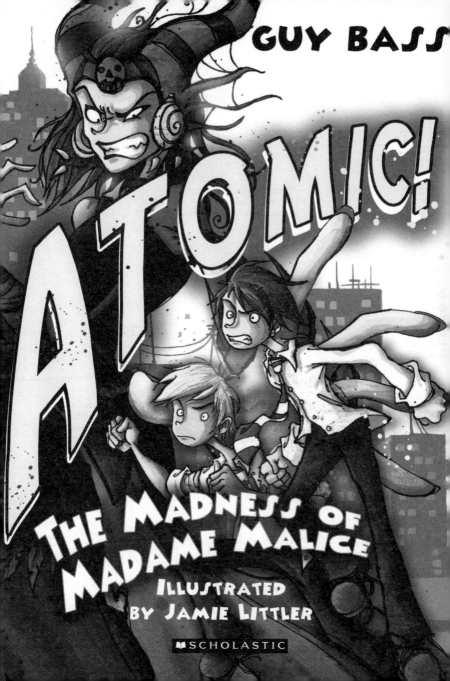

BREAKOUT

Albion City Telegraph

BURSTING AT THE SEAMS?
Mayor promises all is well at The Stronghold

"Nothing can possibly go wrong,"

assures Mayor Johnson

THE NEAR FUTURE

BOOM.

The explosion was heard twenty kilometres away. Mrs Edith Piffle, a seventy-nine-year-old retired florist living in the leafy suburb of Albion Redrose,

1

was so startled by the noise that she dropped a Fondant Fancy on top of her cat, Nosepick.

The cat was unharmed.

"Explosion in Sector 4! The prisoners are escaping!"

Meanwhile, at The Stronghold – Albion City's high-security super-prison – all eighty-eight of its villainous inmates were suddenly free from their cells and racing across the courtyard.

"Report!" cried the chief warden as he looked out of the control tower atop the vast prison walls. "Who in the name of my Great Aunt Edith let out the supervillains?"

"The prisoners have just blown a hole in the prison walls!" replied a panicking prison officer. "They're free . . . and they've got their *powers* back."

"Impossible! What about the power chokers?" snapped the chief warden. "Those collars should reduce their superpowers to nothing!"

"The power chokers aren't working, sir!" cried another officer, frantically pressing buttons on a control panel. "In fact, *nothing's* working – even the generators have shut down!"

"It's called an EMP, you silly boys – an *electro-magnetic pulse*," said a voice. The wardens looked out of the window to see a tall, willowy woman with jet-black hair floating in the air.

"M-Madame Malice!" gasped the chief warden. "P-please don't hurt me!"

"Don't worry, I have *far* more pressing matters to attend to," replied Madame Malice. "Catch me if you can. . ."

Madame Malice launched herself skyward. Within seconds she had vanished into the clouds.

"Now to find my sons," she said, as she soared through the air. "Now to find Tommy and Jonny."

THE PROBLEM WITH BEING ORDINARY

Albion City Telegraph

BREAKOUT AT THE STRONGHOLD!

**Eighty-eight supervillains escape
from Albion City's maximum-security prison**

That moment, in a small classroom in Babblebrook Primary School, a hundred and ninety-nine kilometres east of the prison breakout, two boys were writing an essay entitled "Why I Am an Ant".

Their names were Jonny and Tommy Atomic –

and they were the "secret" sons of the greatest superhero the world had ever known.

"You know what I like about pretending we're ordinary?" said Tommy, shooting his brother a stern glare. "*Nothing*. What is your problem with being *super*, anyway?"

Jonny Atomic stared back at his twin brother. It would have been like looking in a mirror, except that while Jonny's hair was bright blond, Tommy's was jet black and seemed to point scruffily in every direction.

"What do you want me to say? That it's all my fault we're at school?" Jonny whispered. "Fine. I got us into this. But you could make it easier – we've missed lunch twice this week because of you messing around."

"What else am I meant to do?" replied Tommy. "I write every essay and pass every test in record time. All that's left for me to do is wind up old Ms Crackdown."

ATOMIC FILES

NAME: Tommy Atomic

AGE: 10 1/4

EYES: Green

HAIR: Black

POWERS AND ABILITIES:

Level 6.3 Psychic Ability (Telekenesis) — subject can lift, move and repel objects with the power of his mind. Can create psychic force fields and fly at speeds of up to 200 kph. [Note: Subject's Powers inherited from his mother's side (refer to file: Madame Malice).]

Subject also possesses genius-level intellect. Excels in quantum dynamics, materials chemistry and sudoku.

ATOMIC FILES

NAME: Jonny Atomic

AGE: 10 1/4

EYES: Green

HAIR: Blond

POWERS AND ABILITIES:

Level 6 Physical Ability –

super-strength, super-speed

and high resistance to

physical injury. Can toss a tractor 100 metres. [Note A: Have

yet to determine how a tractor got on to Atomic Island in

the first place. Prime suspect: Tommy Atomic.]

[Note B: Subject's Power levels as yet undetermined –

subject seems reluctant to explore the full extent of his

abilities.]

"What are you moaning about?" whispered Jonny. "We've got, like, five hours till half-term. Then you won't have to think about school for a whole week."

"About time, too," beamed Tommy. "Do you really think Dad's going to take some time off work? I mean, he *promised* he was going to do 'dad stuff' with us, but something always seems to get in the—"

"TWIN A! TWIN B!"

came a cry. The boys looked up. Their teacher, Ms Crackdown, had her back to the class as she stared out of the window. She turned to face them, adjusting her impressive bright-red wig as if it were a hat.

"Did I, or did I not, insist upon silence during this lesson?" continued Ms Crackdown. "You may think you're special but in this classroom, you are all *ants*."

ATOMIC FILES

NAME: Anita Crackdown (Ms)

AKA: The Blue Dynamo (former superhero, now retired)

AGE: 59

EYES: Green

HAIR: None (Hair loss an apparent side effect of the subject's superpowers)

DESCRIPTION: Teacher at Jonny and Tommy's school. Former superhero.

POWERS AND ABILITIES: Level 6 Energetic Ability – subject can generate bolts of bioelectricity. [Note: Subject has been out of the "superhero business" for over thirty years. Powers levels may have diminished through lack of use.]

Jonny rolled his eyes. It wasn't that he regretted badgering his dad to let them go to school. He relished the chance to pretend that he was ordinary. But the thought of another day with Ms Crackdown breathing down his neck made him shudder. She was mean to them at the best of times, but since she had discovered their secret identities, she was more horrible than ever.

"What's her problem?" whispered Tommy, when Ms Crackdown returned to staring out of the window. "She used to be *The Blue Dynamo, Defender of the Innocent*. Shouldn't she be nicer to us now she knows we're Atomics?"

"Shhh," replied Jonny. "Don't get me into any more trouble than—"

"I reckon she hates *superheroes* worse than anyone," continued Tommy. "I mean, there's no way *I'd* give up being a superhero to be ordinary.

She must be *bonkers*."

"Would you *shut* up?" growled Jonny . . . a little too loudly.

"TWIN A!" screeched Ms Crackdown. "You're proving to be as troublesome as your brother. Well, you have both earned yet another lunch time under my watchful eye. There now, don't you feel special?"

"Five more hours," sighed Jonny to himself. "Just five more—"

KNOCK-KNOCK!

The whole class turned to the door as it creaked slowly open. A woman's face appeared from behind the door.

"I do beg your pardon, but do I have the correct class? I'm looking for Jonathan and Thomas," said the woman as she stepped into the room. She was tall and lean and wearing a trim black suit.

Jonny and Tommy's jaws dropped. Then they both spoke a single word:

"MUM!"

VISITING RIGHTS

THE ALBION ADVISOR

ATOMIC ALONE?

**Can even Captain Atomic catch
88 supervillains single-handedly?**

Tommy and Jonny stared at their mother. It had
been two years since they'd last seen her. They'd
thought she was locked away in The Stronghold
for trying to take over the world.

ATOMIC FILES

NAME: Madame Malice

ALIASES: Various; alter egos include Millicent Malice, Seraphina Syn, Dahlia D'Eville

AGE: 39

EYES: Black

HAIR: Black

KNOWN RELATIVES: Tommy and Jonny Atomic (sons)

GROUP AFFILIATION: Chaos Inc.

CONVICTIONS: 123 Acts of "Super-Terrorism" (Appendix A.13), including robbery, theft, assault with a double decker bus, assault with a light aircraft, assault with a light aircraft carrier, GPH (grievous psychic harm), attempted mayhem, actual mayhem, actual bodily squashing, attempted world domination.

POWERS AND ABILITIES: Level 9 Psychic Ability (Telekenesis) – Subject is incredibly powerful – can lift, move and repel objects with the power of her mind. Can also create force fields, reshape and reconstruct inanimate matter, fly at high speeds and make trouble wherever she goes.

"My boys!" cried the boys' mother, rushing towards them and giving them a hug. "You're so *big*! Has it been so very long?"

"Mum . . . what are you doing here?" whispered Jonny through gritted teeth.

"Interruptions are not acceptable!" snarled Ms Crackdown. "If you wish to consort with one of the insects, I suggest you wait until three thirty. Now, I insist you leave *immediately*."

"Don't be silly," said Madame Malice. She waved her hand and Ms Crackdown fell back into her chair. She struggled to get up, but was fixed to the spot.

"What in the world—" began Ms Crackdown, but with another wave of the woman's hand, her mouth clamped shut.

"Hush," added the boys' mother. "Now then, I think two such distinguished pupils can afford to miss a day of school, wouldn't you agree?"

"Gmph-mmph-mph!" Ms Crackdown groaned.

"I'll take that as a yes," said Madame Malice. "Come along, my dears – we've got *so* much catching up to do."

"I don't think—" began Jonny, but Tommy interrupted with "Great!" and hurried them out of the classroom.

A minute later, Madame Malice was sitting with her two sons under a tree on Babblebrook village green. She hugged them so tightly they could hardly breathe.

"My boys, my wonderful boys. . ."

"How did you get out of prison?" asked Tommy, excitedly.

"How do you think?" said Jonny. "She *broke* out."

"Only so that I could see you, my little canary – and you, my wonderful little raven!" replied the boys' mum. "It wasn't easy – there were months of planning. The key was finding a way to deactivate the power chokers. Once I had my powers back, I could blow that prison to smithereens. . ."

"But how did you find us?" asked Tommy.

"Oh, I knew your father would send you to school sooner or later – and it's not easy hiding identical twins in the education system," replied the boys' mother. "All I had to do was *find* you. It's amazing what you can accomplish if you put your mind to it – even from prison."

"You shouldn't have looked for us," said Jonny, trying to sound like he meant it. "If Dad finds you, he'll send you straight back."

"Don't worry, my little canary," replied Madame Malice. "I suspect your father's going to be kept busy for a while, tracking down all those escaped supervillains."

"What's your problem, Jonny?" said Tommy.

"Mum has risked a lot coming to see us!"

"I haven't got a problem!" snapped Jonny. "I just don't know if this is a good idea."

"Now, now – I don't want you falling out," said their mum, softly. "You have to look after each other. No one will ever *know* you like you know each other. Not . . . not even me."

"Mum. . ." said Tommy.

"But I'd *like* to," continued Madame Malice. "That's what I came here to tell you. I had a lot of time to think in prison – about what I've done . . . what I've missed. You see, I didn't escape so that I could try to take over the world. I did it so I could see *you*. All I really want is to be a *mum* again. If you'll only give me the chance, I'll—"

"Get away from those boys!" came a cry. Ms Crackdown was racing across the school car park towards the village green.

"It's our teacher! Mum, get out of here!" blurted Tommy.

"She's tougher than she looks – *psychic paralysis* usually lasts longer," huffed Madame Malice, and raised her arms. "Still, a tree in the face should slow her down. . ."

"What? No, wait!" begged Jonny. "Please, Mum – our secret identities. . ."

Madame Malice paused for a moment.

"You're right, of course. Once a supervillain, always a supervillain!" she said with a smile. "Tell you what, you promise to keep our little meetings a secret and I promise not to throw a tree at your teacher."

"How is that even a fair—" began Jonny.

"Deal!" interrupted Tommy.

"Super!" cried the boys' mum. "I'll come for you tomorrow. So, where is that invisible island of yours?"

"Uh, we're not supposed to say," replied Jonny.

"What is wrong with you?" snapped Tommy, jabbing Jonny again. "Mum just wants to see us, she's not going to—"

"No, Jonny's right to be cautious," interrupted their mother. "Not to worry – look for my signal."

THE SIGNAL

THE ALBION EYE

HELP ON THE WAY?

HEROES FLY IN FROM NEIGHBOURING
CITIES TO HELP WITH THE STRONGHOLD
SUPERVILLAIN CRISIS

*Miss Mystery, Mr V and
The Unknown Quantity pledge their
superheroic support to Captain Atomic –
but will it be enough?*

This was the longest Jonny and Tommy's mother
had been in prison – usually they could expect a
visit every few months, when her fellow villains in
Chaos Inc. sprang their leader from captivity. The

boys wondered how long it would be before their dad recaptured the villains. They both decided to keep their end of the bargain – neither of them mentioned seeing their mother.

As the boys tucked into their breakfast, a small black dog with a salt-and-pepper beard trotted into the room.

"I'm afraid any half-term plans will have to be put on hold," noted the dog.

"THOSE EIGHTY–EIGHT SUPERVILLAINS AREN'T GOING TO RECAPTURE THEMSELVES. . ."

"I'm sure you can find plenty to occupy yourselves on the Island!" said their aunt, who happened to be a super-intelligent brown and white hamster.

ATOMIC FILES

NAME: Uncle Dogday

AGE: 63 (Dog years)

EYES: Brown

HAIR: Black and grey

POWERS AND ABILITIES:

Scientifically-increased intelligence and the ability to speak.
Expert in quantum mechanics, radar, computer hacking,
fetching and "playing dead".

ATOMIC FILES

NAME: Aunt Sandwich

AGE: 44 (Hamster years)

EYES: Brown

HAIR: Brown and white

POWERS AND ABILITIES:

Subject has scientifically-increased intelligence and the ability to speak.

Qualified Atomic Bomber pilot.

Concert pianist (toy pianos only).

"Has Dad been in touch?" asked Jonny. He stared up at the control room's numerous view screens. It was a view he'd never seen before – of a city overrun with supervillains.

"He's battling Agony Ant and his Drones in the east district," replied Uncle Dogday.

"Just another day at the office!" joked Aunt Sandwich.

"Uncle Dogday?" began Tommy, quietly. "Do you think a villain could ever turn . . . good?"

Jonny bristled. Was Tommy trying to tell them about their mother?

"Well, of course it's possible," answered Uncle Dogday. "Indeed, I know a number of reformed villains – Alpha Male, Smash 'n' Grab, The Phantoman. . ."

"Really? All of them turned out to be heroes?" said Tommy.

"Well, not quite. . . It turned out Alpha Male

was just *pretending* to be heroic, and Smash 'n' Grab wound up back in prison for smashing and grabbing, and The Phantoman *did* turn the whole of Bastion City into a ghost town . . . but I'm sure it works out occasionally."

"Just because someone isn't doing evil stuff right now doesn't make them—" began Jonny, before he noticed something odd in one of the view screens.

Above Albion City's tallest skyscraper a strange shape was forming – a thick, dark cloud of dust. It churned in the air as if it were alive. Finally, the shape of a skull emerged in the darkness.

"The signal!" he whispered. He gave Tommy a sharp kick under the table.

"OW! Are you trying to break my leg?" snapped Tommy. Jonny didn't reply, he just nodded at the view screen. Tommy turned and gasped.

"Are you all right, Tommy?" asked Aunt Sandwich.

"Just off to the recreation centre going to watch some cartoons probably be busy all day see you later come on Jonny!" he said in a single breath.

He grabbed Jonny and rushed out of the room.

"Oh me, oh my! Don't you want to finish your breakfast?" squeaked Aunt Sandwich . . . but the boys were gone.

ESCAPING THE ISLAND

Albion City Telegraph

WAR ZONE

**Areas of Albion City declared unsafe
as escaped supervillains run riot**

"She came back!" cried Tommy as they raced through the Island. "That signal . . . she's in the city!"

"Yeah, really subtle. I'm sure no one else has noticed the *giant skull-shaped dust cloud* in the sky. . ." said Jonny.

"How else is she going to reach us? You wouldn't even tell her where we are!" snapped Tommy.

"Fat lot of good it does us – you know the rules," replied Jonny. "Dad said we're not allowed to leave the Island unless we're with a responsible adult or animal. . ."

"Mum's a responsible adult," said Tommy.

"She tried to take over the world!"

"That was *ages* ago," said Tommy, running towards a nearby lift. "Anyway, they won't even know we're gone."

"Seriously? How do you plan on getting off the Island?" asked Jonny. "It's not like we can just borrow an Atomic Bomber."

"Duh, I can *fly*, remember?" replied Tommy. He shoved Jonny into the lift and pressed a button. A sign under it read:

⁎⁎TO ISLAND EXTERIOR⁎⁎
⁎⁎DANGER HIGH ALTITUDE⁎⁎
⁎⁎ATMOSPHERE NOT BREATHABLE⁎⁎

"No way! We're miles above the surface! The air is too thin up here to breathe," said Jonny as the lift doors slid closed.

"You are *such* a baby," huffed Tommy. "I can create a pocket of air around us – you'll be fine."

"We're not doing this," said Jonny, his hand hovering over the lift's HOLD button. "Dad'll kill us."

"Look, if you want to stay, *stay*. Stay here and do what you're told *for ever*," replied Tommy. "But I'm going to see Mum."

Jonny tried to pretend that going with Tommy would be a good way of keeping him out of trouble, but the fact was, he really wanted to see his mother, too.

"OK. Just for a few minutes," he said.

"That's more like it," grinned Tommy, enveloping them in an air bubble. "Stay close so I can keep the bubble tight. And brace yourself – it's a bit *breezy* up here."

The lift door opened on to the Island's surface. The freezing air roared around them. Tommy grabbed his brother's arm and raced towards the Island's edge.

"READY?" yelled Tommy as he peered over the edge at the city far below.

"NOT REALLY!" screamed Jonny, the wind whistling around his head.

"YOU BIG BABY!" shouted Tommy – as they jumped!

"Y A A A A A H!"

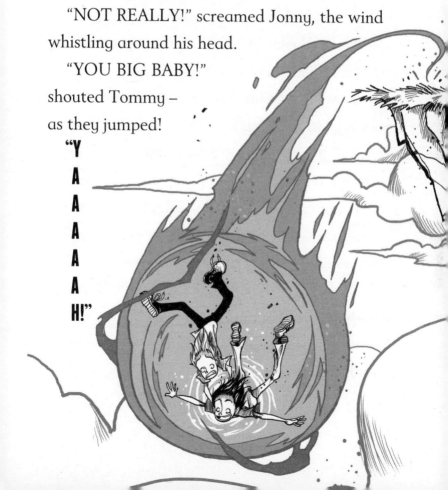

THE RETURN OF MADAME MALICE

Albion Today
YOUR CITY'S LOCAL E-PAPER

GOING UNDERGROUND
Fears that some supervillains will disappear without a trace – but can they resist causing mayhem?

Tommy and Jonny passed through the imperceptors' invisibility shield and plummeted towards the city.

"Fly! Fly!" yelled Jonny as the city raced up towards them. "Tommy! Do it NOW!"

Tommy chuckled as he finally flew them both high into the air.

"Can't you fly in a straight line? I'm going to throw up!" barked Jonny as they headed for the skull cloud. And there, atop the highest skyscraper in Albion City—

"Mum!" cried Tommy as he landed on the skyscraper's roof, dropping Jonny with a less-than-gentle THUD.

Jonny quickly scrambled to his feet and looked up. He gasped at the sight of Madame Malice, dressed in her grand supervillain attire. She wore a long black and crimson robe, with a huge headdress that looked like devilish horns.

In the centre of the headdress was a distinctive skull emblem. Madame Malice waved an arm and her skull signal immediately dissolved in the air.

"My boys!" she cried in delight. "And under your own steam. Your powers are really coming along. . ."

"Dad says my psychics are up to Level six point three," said Tommy. "And he says I'm brainier than he was at my age."

"The best of both worlds! What a clever boy!" she laughed, kissing Tommy on the head. "And how about you, Jonathan?"

"I—" began Jonny.

"Jonny's a *tank*," said Tommy. "Strong like Dad but without the brains."

"Shut up, Tommy!" snapped Jonny. "I'm Level six too! I just don't show off about it."

"Levels. . ." sighed the boys' mother, shaking her head. "Your powers are a wonderful gift, not something to be ranked or graded. Honestly, your father treats your powers like *schoolwork*."

"Yeah, and when we're not doing that, we're doing *actual* schoolwork," grumbled Tommy.

"Well, I'm going to show you how to make the most of your powers," said Madame Malice. "The world is your *playground*. You shouldn't be trapped on some silly island. You should be showing everyone what you're capable of. You should be free!"

"Finally!" grinned Tommy.

"But Dad says it's best that no one knows about us," said Jonny. "He says it's for our own safety."

"I hate to admit it, but your father has a point," smirked Madame Malice. "There are some fairly despicable supervillains who would love to take advantage of the fact that Captain Atomic has a weakness."

"We're *not* a weakness!" said Tommy, firmly.

"Of course not, my little raven," said Madame Malice. "But the point is, why hide you away? You have secret identities at school, so why not have *super secret* identities? Here, I have something for you. . ."

Madame Malice reached into her robe and took out two crimson masks. Each one was emblazoned with the same distinctive skull emblem as she wore on her headdress.

"Put these on and no one will recognize you," she said.

"This teeny little mask? It barely even covers our eyes," said Jonny.

"Trust me, it works," she replied. "Now then, let's have some *fun*! Who wants ice cream?"

ONE SCOOP OF ICE CREAM, TWO SCOOPS OF VILLAINY?

Icy Joe's Delectable Dairy Den (and Fantabulous Flavour Funhouse) was the best ice-cream parlour in Albion City. Icy Joe prided himself on one thousand and fifty-four adventurous ice cream flavours, including Banana Bacon Blend-a-thon,

Mango Mint Mousetrap, Choco-cheese Sneeze and Sparkling Strawberry Spaghetti Sauce.

"Dad would never let us come here," said Tommy as they hovered above the giant ice-cream-shaped building.

"What your father doesn't know can't bother him, can it?" chuckled Madame Malice.

"What if he finds out?" asked Jonny, adjusting his mask. "I mean, what if someone saw your signal?"

"Why, that's all part of the fun, my little canary," laughed Madame Malice. "So, what flavour would you like?"

"Crazy Crispy Custard-Mustard Combo!" cried Tommy.

"Coming up!" said Madame Malice, and raised her arms. Bystanders looked up to see the roof shudder and shake, before it was torn from the building! Madame Malice flew herself into the Dairy Den and landed next to the counter as the salesperson cowered in fear.

"Three double Crazy Crispy Custard-Mustard Combos, if you wouldn't mind," said Madame Malice. "And don't be stingy with the Slippery Sprinkles."

*

Moments later, Madame Malice and her boys hovered above Albion City Lake, licking ice cream as their toes dangled in the water.

"What about Icy Joe?" asked Jonny, quietly. "He can't make ice cream without a roof on his shop."

Madame Malice smiled.

"Old habits die hard. I may not want to take over the world, but I am what I am!" she replied. "Anyway, doesn't it feel nice to be yourselves for once, instead of pretending to be ordinary?"

"But Dad says we only have our superpowers so we can help people," said Jonny, a little awkwardly.

"So how come he keeps us locked away on the Island?" grumped Tommy. "How come he never lets us use our powers to do anything? It's like he's *ashamed* of us. . ."

"Well I'm not ashamed! I'm proud of my remarkable boys!" cried Madame Malice. "Why don't we try something different? Why don't we try to have some *fun*?"

THE PROMISE

SUPER!

YOUR DAILY SUPERHERO GOSSIP COLUMN
Don't catch 'em, Cap!

Life's so much more fun
with supervillains
on the loose!

For the rest of the day, Madame Malice
showed the boys exactly what
they'd been missing
by being stuck on
Atomic Island,
including:

- *A trip to the zoo.*

Madame Malice decided to open all the enclosures so the animals could "be free". Even Jonny chuckled at the sight of the zookeeper being chased by a confused giraffe.

- *A visit to the museum.*

Madame Malice wasn't interested in teaching the boys about history, but she did show them how much fun it was to make it seem that the dinosaur skeletons had come to life. A Tyrannosaurus skeleton pursuing a horde of terrified museum-goers down the street was *really* something.

• *An outing to the park.*

Albion City Park served as the perfect arena for a duel of epic proportions! While Captain Atomic discouraged the boys from fighting, Madame Malice thought it was a great idea. Every time the boys expected to hear, "Stop roughhousing!" they heard their mother cry, "Take no prisoners! Kick him in the shins! FIGHT!"

Both boys felt a bit guilty at having so much fun – they knew their dad wouldn't approve . . . but it somehow felt like they deserved it after all those years stuck on Atomic Island.

It was late afternoon before the boys' mother said sadly, "Better call it a day, I suppose. Don't want anyone wondering where you've got to."

"Where's *your* home?" asked Tommy.

"The middle of a volcano, of course," said Madame Malice, nonchalantly. "Bit clichéd for a supervillain, but molten lava has its advantages. Low heating bills, mainly."

"When do we get to see you again?" asked Tommy.

"I'm your mother," smiled Madame Malice. "I'm not going *anywhere*."

A hug later and the boys' mother disappeared into the clouds. The boys stood in stunned silence for a long moment.

"That . . . was AWESOME!" cried Tommy, finally. "I had no idea how *small* that stupid island was until I was out here with Mum."

"It *was* fun," admitted Jonny. "But do you think

maybe we should tell Dad? About Mum, I mean?"

Tommy stared at Jonny.

"Don't you dare," said Tommy, finally. "Don't you *dare* ruin this for me."

"I'm not!" replied Jonny. "Anyway, you try to ruin school for me every day. . ."

"Wait, is this about school?" snapped Tommy. "School is stupid! It's just Ms Crackdown whining about us being ants. It couldn't be more stupid if *you* were headmaster! This is our mum! And you *promised* not to say anything."

"I know," said Jonny. "I just—"

"Promise again. Right now," said Tommy, gripping Jonny in a force field until he lifted him off his feet. "**SUPER ATOMIC PROMISE** that you won't tell. Do it!"

"All right! I promise," mumbled Jonny. The thought of betraying his mum bothered him almost as much as lying to his dad.

The whole thing made his head hurt.

"Good," said Tommy, placing Jonny back on his feet. "You'll see. This is going to be the best half-term *ever*."

THE FATE OF BABBLEBROOK SCHOOL

THE ALBION OBSERVER

Mayor Resigns over Prison Escape

Admits Stronghold "Wasn't Strong Enough"

The week that followed wasn't just "the best half-term ever" – it was probably the best week of Tommy and Jonny's entire lives. With their dad, Uncle Dogday and Aunt Sandwich busily tracking down escaped supervillains, it was easy for the boys to sneak away for a few hours every day and meet up with their mother.

Until now, most of their adventures in the outside world had been frustratingly brief – and had always had some sort of "educational value". But spending time with their mother was exciting, spur-of-the-moment and utterly *wild*.

Each day offered them a new adventure to Albion City and far beyond – flights of fancy to far-off continents, races and chases and good old-fashioned fights.

Behind their masks it was easy for the boys to enjoy themselves (and occasionally break stuff) without fear of getting into trouble. It was just like their mother had said – the whole world was their playground. Even Jonny, who had longed to be ordinary, started to love his mother's carefree outlook on life.

By Sunday, however, a dark cloud loomed over their heads. A cloud in the shape of Ms Crackdown.

"I can't believe we have to go to school tomorrow," groaned Tommy, watching the sun dip behind Albion City's skyline from the top of their favourite skyscraper. "Back to Ms Crackdown calling us ants and being *horrible*. I'm not sure I can go back to being ordinary."

"I'll tell you what: why don't I pay you a visit tomorrow at school?" said Madame Malice. "I can bring you your present."

"A present? Cool! What is it?" asked Tommy.

"You'll see," chuckled Madame Malice, kissing Tommy on the head. "Now, bedtime. Would you like a lift home?"

"Yeah, that'd be—" began Tommy.

"Uh, better not," interrupted Jonny, guiltily. "Secret base . . . sorry."

"Still my cautious little canary," she said and kissed Jonny goodbye. "Well, then – until tomorrow."

And with that, she was a dot in the sky.

"You are *such* an idiot," said Tommy. "Mum only escaped from prison because of us. Would it kill you to trust her for, like, a second?"

"I do! I do, but. . ." replied Jonny.

"Forget it," huffed Tommy. "Don't worry, we'll be back in your favourite place tomorrow – *school*."

As it happened, Monday morning couldn't come quickly enough for Tommy – even if it did mean going to school. He couldn't wait to see his mother again.

"Oh me, oh my, I hope your dad makes it back for tea tonight – he must be dying for some home-cooked food," said Aunt Sandwich as she piloted the boys to school.

"Yeah," muttered Tommy. He peered out of the bomber window, hoping to catch sight of some signal from his mother. His brother sat back in his chair, listening to the hum of the Atomic Bomber's engine, wondering if he would ever be able to tell his dad about Madame Malice.

That was when Jonny noticed a plume of smoke rising into the air in the distance.

By the time he'd said, "Tommy, look!" the super-fast Atomic Bomber was already touching down on Babblebrook village green.

The smoke was coming from the school.

"Oh me . . . oh MY!"

Or rather, what was *left* of the school.

"Oh, no," whispered Jonny.

Where once stood the school, there was nothing but smouldering rubble. Babblebrook Primary had been totally destroyed.

Police cars and fire engines surrounded the wreckage, along with hysterical parents, children and onlookers.

"Chestnuts! What happened to the school?" squeaked Aunt Sandwich.

"We'll deal with this, Aunt Sandwich," said Tommy, confidently. "You get back to the Island . . . see if you can find out anything about what happened here!"

"Well, I think I should probably—" began Aunt Sandwich.

"We'll keep a low profile – scope out the place," added Tommy. "You trust us, right?"

It didn't take much more prodding to convince Aunt Sandwich that she could do more good on Atomic Island than she could in Babblebrook.

"What was that all about?" asked Jonny as they raced across the village green.

"I think I know what happened," said Tommy. "And if I'm right. . ."

"So, do you like your present?" said a voice. Jonny and Tommy spun around to see their mother, dressed in her civilian attire.

"I knew it!" said Tommy.

"Wait, *you* did this?" whispered Jonny through gritted teeth.

"No need to thank me – it's just nice to be able to give my boys what they want," chuckled

Madame Malice. "And now you have no excuse not to spend time with your mother!"

Tommy stared at the rubble in silence.

"Mum, what have you done?" growled Jonny. "You can't just go around wrecking schools! It's not right!"

"But – but you said you didn't want to go back," replied Madame Malice, a little taken aback. "I thought I was *helping*."

"How is this helping?" snapped Jonny. "What about the teachers and the pupils? What if someone got hurt?"

"Of course I made sure no one was inside. . . I – I thought this was what you wanted." said Madame Malice, imploringly.

"It's OK, Mum," said Tommy, putting his hand on her arm. "You were . . . trying to help. I guess these things happen."

"*How do 'these things happen'?*" snarled Jonny,

grabbing Tommy and pulling him aside. "We can't keep doing this. I mean, look around!"

"What is wrong with you? Can't you see you're upsetting Mum?" growled Tommy. "OK, maybe she went overboard. Maybe it wasn't the way you'd do it or the way Dad does things, but she was trying to do something for us!"

"Tommy – Mum is a *supervillain*!" said Jonny, clenching his fist. "She tried to take over the world!"

"Yeah, you've said – a *million* times," replied Tommy. "Well, guess what? She can't be taking over the world when she's with us, can she? So maybe us all being together is the best thing that can happen. Maybe this way we can help her to be better. Maybe this way no one has to take over the world and no one has to save it! Did you think about that?"

"I don't – I . . ." began Jonny, but part of him

knew Tommy was right. As long as Madame Malice was with them, she couldn't be doing anything *that* evil. Jonny sighed and shook his head.

"So *stop* giving her a hard time," said Tommy. "Mum's on *our* side."

"NOOOOOOO!" came a cry.

"Is that. . .? Ms Crackdown?" asked Tommy. Their teacher was running across the lawn towards the school.

"Oh dear," sighed their mother, shaking her head. "If you're not happy with the school, then you probably won't be pleased about this either. . ."

"What did you do?" asked Jonny, not looking forward to the answer.

"I may have found out where Ms Crackdown lived. . ." said Madame Malice, quietly. "And sort of flattened her *house*, too."

"You did *what*?" cried Jonny.

"You said she was horrible! I mean, she called you ants!" replied Madame Malice. "I thought it might teach her a lesson. . ."

"You!" cried Ms Crackdown as she raced towards them. "You . . . I know you!"

"We should go – *now*," said Jonny, firmly.

"Yeah, as far away as possible," added Tommy. "*North Pole* far."

"What a marvellous idea!" replied Madame Malice. "I haven't been to the North Pole in *ages*."

SECRETS (AND SECRET ORIGINS)

THE BABBLEBROOK BABBLE

SQUASHED SCHOOL "ONE OF THOSE THINGS"

SAY RESIDENTS

"Worse things happen at sea," says man

with two wooden legs

A few hours of breathtaking, hyper-speed flight later, and the boys and their mother found themselves in the frozen wastelands of the North Pole. Jonny and his mother watched Tommy chase a polar bear around in the snow and pelt it with snowballs.

"Are you cold, my little canary?" asked Madame Malice.

"No – I don't really feel it till minus fifty degrees," replied Jonny. He sighed and watched a cloud of breath disappear into the air.

"I'm sorry I shouted at you," he added. "I know you were trying to help."

"No, *I'm* sorry – I messed up again," said Madame Malice. "I'm a supervillain. I've always been a supervillain, and I probably always will be. People like your father are just . . . *good*. But me . . . well, I am what I am."

"How did you meet Dad?" asked Jonny.

"Ha! There's a story," replied his mother. "I bet he's never told you, has he?"

"Umm," said Jonny. "He doesn't really talk about you . . . ever."

"When I first met your father, I was using a secret identity. And *so was he*."

"But Dad doesn't *have* a secret identity," replied Jonny. "Everyone in the whole world knows who he is."

"It was a *phase* he was going through. He wanted to see what it was like to be *ordinary*," she continued. "He used a disguise. He changed his hairstyle, put on a pair of glasses . . . you'd be surprised what a difference it makes. I met him at a book group – didn't recognize him at all! We got on like a house on fire and both pretended so *brilliantly* that it was months before we found out we were arch-enemies . . . by which time it was too late. Not long after, you boys came along. My greatest achievements."

"I didn't know he wanted to be ordinary," said Jonny, quietly.

"I think he just wanted a holiday from *superheroics*," replied Jonny's mother. "And what do *you* want to be when you grow up, Jonathan?"

"A superhero, I suppose," shrugged Jonny. "Like Dad."

"But is that what you *want* to be?" asked his mother.

"I – I don't know. Sometimes I want to be ordinary, too," Jonny replied.

"And is that why you hold back?" asked his mother.

"What – what do you mean?" asked Jonny.

"I've seen you in action. You're stronger than you pretend," said Madame Malice. "Stronger than Tommy . . . perhaps even stronger than your father. But you're so worried that everyone expects you to be the next Captain Atomic that you stop yourself. You hold back. Am I right?"

"I don't know . . . maybe," muttered Jonny.

"Ten years old and already so responsible!"

laughed his mother. "Jonny, I have no doubt that you will follow in your father's footsteps – and make him proud. But Tommy is different. He's not like you."

"What do you mean?" asked Jonny.

"Tommy wants to be free," continued Madame Malice. "If he stays with your father he's going to realize, sooner or later, that he's not cut out for superheroics. You can see how much happier he is without *responsibilities*. He prefers to do his own thing . . . and that's all being a supervillain really is."

"But Tommy's not a supervillain," said Jonny. He looked over to see Tommy juggling polar bears.

"He deserves to make that choice for himself," she continued. "And that's why I'm going to ask Thomas to be my SIDEKICK."

"Your – your what?" asked Jonny.

"You're an Atomic, my little canary – you always will be," said Madame Malice. "But Tommy . . . Tommy is a MALICE."

CRASH LANDING

ALBION CITY SUN SAYS:

ATOMIC BOMBS
So-called hero fails to keeps streets safe
26 villains still at large after a more than a
week – is Captain Atomic past his prime?

Later that night, when the boys were safely back on Atomic Island, Jonny went to his room and lay on his bed. His head pounded with questions. Should he tell Tommy what Madame Malice had told him? What would that mean? Would Tommy accept the offer to be his mum's sidekick? Would he leave the Island? Would they be *enemies*? And did it mean his mother *preferred* Tommy to him?

VOOT!

VOOT!

VOOT!

The Island's clanging, computerized alarm suddenly blared out in every corner of the Island.

"Proximity alarm activated. Object incoming. Brace for impact."

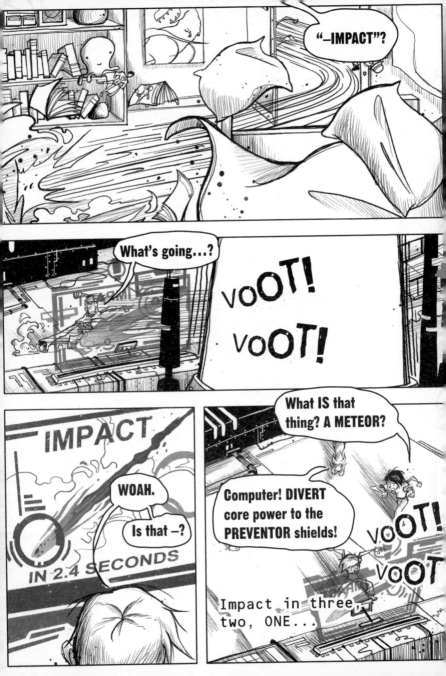

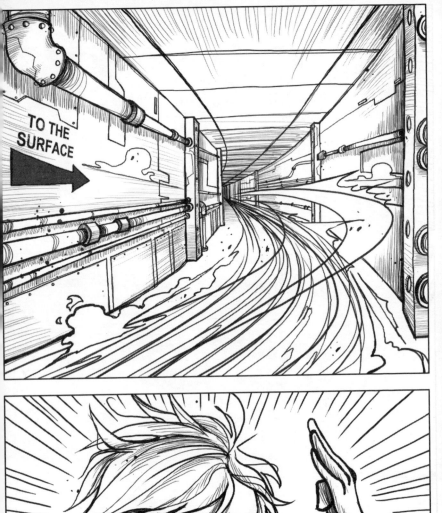

Jonny picked up his still-flaming father and raced him inside. A total of eight seconds passed before he placed Captain Atomic on the floor of the control room.

"Dad! Is he OK?" screamed Tommy as Jonny patted out the last of the flames on his costume. The boys' father, though no longer alight, was charred and smouldering. His flight suit was shredded and his rocket pack (or what was left of it) fizzed and spluttered on his back.

"Don't . . . panic . . . I'm fine," grunted Captain Atomic, dragging himself to his feet. He threw off his rocket pack and winced in pain. He was covered in cuts and bruises and had a week's worth of stubble. "Sorry about . . . the dramatic entrance. Doc Damage blasted my rocket pack back in Albion City . . . fuel caught fire . . . on the way home."

"Oh me, oh my – what a state you're in!" said

Aunt Sandwich. "I'll fetch the first-aid kit and perhaps you'd care for a plate of my award-winning spaghetti Bolognese?"

"That . . . would be nice," said Captain Atomic.

JONNY BREAKS HIS PROMISE

Albion Times

BADDIES GOOD FOR BUSINESS?

City sees 45% rise in tourism as "super-spotters"
try to catch sight of their favourite hero or villain
"I saw Captain Atomic punch Vinister Vile!
In the face!" remarks a happy spotter

An hour later, a showered and bandaged Captain
Atomic sat in his dressing gown, tucking into his
fifth bowl of spaghetti Bolognese as the rest of the
family looked on.

"Baron Blastoff wrecked my Atomic Bomber –
I've been using my rocket pack to get around. I

didn't realize Doc Damage had done so much . . . damage," he said between mouthfuls. "Oh, and Bounceback reflected my multi-gun's shrink ray back at it – look."

Captain Atomic reached into his holster and took out his multi-gun. It had been shrunk to the size of a penny.

"Oh me, oh my! It's hamster-sized!" giggled Aunt Sandwich, wielding the tiny weapon.

"Well, I'll need a full-sized one from the armoury," continued Captain Atomic. "There's no time to lose."

"Captain, you've been battling supervillains non-stop for nearly ten days," said Uncle Dogday. "Don't you think it's high time you had a well-earned rest?"

"I've still got twenty-six supervillains to track down," replied Captain Atomic. "The Planetoid and Doctor Different are planning to destroy the city's power grid. Then I'll need to deal with General Disorder and The Antagonist. Power Punch and Judo Judy said they'd try to bring down Alpha Male, but those two are *bound* to need rescuing. . ."

Jonny felt a shiver down his spine. Was this the life his mum had planned for Tommy? Being pursued by superheroes? Being hunted by his own dad? Was Tommy going to end up in prison?

Captain Atomic dragged himself up from the table and began striding towards the Bomber hangar bay. Then he stopped and turned around.

"Sorry boys, I never asked. How was half-term?"

Jonny and Tommy looked at each other.

"Fine," said Tommy. "We stayed hidden away on the Island, just like you wanted."

Captain Atomic stared at Tommy.

"I have to go," he said, finally.

"We saw *Mum*!" Jonny blurted out. Everyone froze.

"Do you mean you saw her on the view screens?" Captain Atomic was gritting his teeth.

"I mean, we met up with her. . . a bunch of times, in Albion City," admitted Jonny.

"Jonny!" growled Tommy.

"Did you know about this?" Captain Atomic asked, glaring at Uncle Dogday and Aunt Sandwich.

"Oh me, oh my, no! This is the first we've heard!" cried Aunt Sandwich. "I mean, we've been so busy, but . . . the boys never leave the Island without us – do they?"

"What are you doing?" whispered Tommy.

"I'm – I'm sorry," replied Jonny. He took a deep breath and said, "Mum says she wants to make Tommy a supervillain. She wants him to be her *sidekick*."

"She said that?" said Tommy and Captain Atomic together.

"She told me yesterday, at the North Pole," Jonny muttered. "She said Tommy is a *Malice*."

"You went to the *North Pole*?" cried Uncle Dogday.

"*Sidekick. . .*" muttered Tommy, a smile spreading across his face.

"And neither of you thought to mention the fact that your – that Madame Malice was visiting you on a regular basis?" snarled Captain Atomic.

"You weren't here to tell. . ." said Tommy, quietly.

"What kind of an excuse is that? I'm sorry I have been working a lot recently, but someone has to keep the world safe!" growled Captain Atomic. "I can see I need to keep a closer eye on you both. Dogday, lock down the whole island. No one gets in – or *out*."

"What difference does that make? This island is like a prison anyway. It's *always* been a prison!" shouted Tommy. "Mum lets us do what we want!"

"She's trying to turn you into a supervillain!" snapped Jonny.

"You're just jealous because she chose *me* to be her sidekick instead of you!" shouted Tommy.

"That's not true!" replied Jonny.

"It *is* true!" yelled Tommy. "You're jealous because Mum loves me more than you!"

"Tommy Atomic, that's enough!" barked Uncle Dogday.

"Anything would be better than being stuck on this stupid island," Tommy growled, tears welling up in his eyes. "I'm sick of it. I'm sick of you! I'm sick of everything!"

"Tommy. . ." said Aunt Sandwich, softly.

"Dogday, Sandwich – please make sure Tommy and Jonny stay in their rooms," said Captain Atomic. "I don't want them leaving the Island – not even to go to school."

"You can't even *send* us to school!" said Tommy, victoriously. "Mum smashed it to pieces. It's nothing but a pile of bricks!"

"In that case," said Captain Atomic, grimly, "you have no reason to go anywhere, *ever again*. You're grounded."

ESCAPE FROM ATOMIC ISLAND

HAVE CHAOS INC. TURNED OVER A NEW LEAF?
No sign of the world's most dangerous supervillain team since their escape

That night, Tommy Atomic escaped from Atomic Island.

Grounded or not, nothing was going to keep

him there. He felt betrayed by his brother, let down by his father and totally, utterly trapped. More importantly, he had to know the truth – had his mother really chosen him to be her sidekick?

Even with the whole island on

LOCKDOWN

it wasn't hard for Tommy to sneak away. He used his powers to prise off the air-vent cover in his room. Then he slipped into the air duct and followed it to the Island's surface. He crept out into the howling wind as dusk fell. A moment later, he took to the air.

Tommy had no idea of where he was going. He dived into the city, landing on top of his mother's favourite skyscraper. He stared down at the streets below. People scurried and swarmed in the streets as they hurried home.

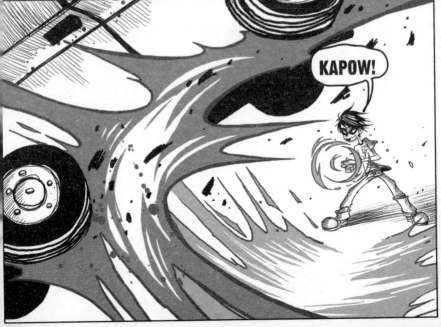

Captain Atomic was battling General Disorder when Uncle Dogday heard of yet another disturbance in Albion City. He brought up the live news feed on the view screen.

"I'm here in the middle of Main Street with one of the stranger reports since The Stronghold breakout," said the reporter. "Hard to believe, but eyewitnesses are saying they saw a *child* crash into the middle of the street and start causing mayhem. . ."

Uncle Dogday's jaw dropped. He ran upstairs to Tommy's room and pressed the door release with his paw. It remained firmly shut.

"Tommy! Open the door this instant! Tommy? Are you in there?" he barked. Jonny appeared from his own room.

"What's happened?" he asked.

"Jonny, I wonder if you'd be so good as to kick

down this door," asked Uncle Dogday.

"Uh, OK," replied Jonny,

"BUT DON'T TAKE IT OUT OF MY POCKET MONEY."

CHAOS INCORPORATED

Within an hour of leaving Albion City, Tommy and his mother were soaring over a moonlit ocean. They had already decided on his new code name – *Kid Malice* – and that his new bedroom was going to have at least two televisions and three games consoles.

"And a freezer full of ice cream!" continued Tommy. "And a bed shaped like a racing car! And a swimming pool!"

"Whatever you want, my little raven," laughed Madame Malice.

"Thanks, Mum," giggled Tommy. He stared out at the open sea. "Are we nearly there yet?"

"Since you ask . . . again," smiled Madame Malice, "yes we are – *look*."

Tommy squinted into the darkness. He could just make out what looked like an island in the water. Then he saw it – in the centre of the island. . .

"A VOLCANO!"

"What did I tell you? No self-respecting supervillain is complete without a secret volcano hideout," chuckled Madame Malice. "I call it Chaos Rock!"

Tommy followed his mother through a concealed entrance at the base of the volcano. They emerged inside a cavernous chamber, with latticed steel girders and walkways leading far into the shadows. In the centre of the space was a large table emblazoned with Madame Malice's skull symbol.

"So, what do you think of your new home?"

"AWESOME!"

cried Tommy. "I can't believe you live here! This is better than *twenty* invisible floating islands!"

"You think *this* is cool?" smiled Madame Malice. "Wait till you meet your *new family*. Front and centre, gentlemen!"

"Family? What do you—" began Tommy, as four strange figures emerged from the shadows.

ATOMIC FILES

CODE NAME: Chaos Incorporated

MEMBERS: Madame Malice (chairperson and founder), Force Face, Cold Shoulder, Creature Features, Gunk

AIMS AND OBJECTIVES: To create mayhem, disorder, carnage and litter wherever they go

CONVICTIONS: More than 200, including robbery, assault, public disorder, extortion, acts of extreme beastliness, cold-hearted criminality and grievous bodily gunking

"So, this is the kid, huh?" said the first figure. He had a large FF on his chest, and his entire face was plated with grey armour. He leaned down until he was reinforced-nose-to-nose with Tommy, and tapped his cheek with a *TUNK TUNK TUNK!*

"They call me Force Face. This here is reinforced endurium. Totally unbreakable. I can smash it through *anything.*"

"Cool. . ." muttered Tommy.

"*Cool* indeed!" said the second figure. He was a slender man and seemed to be made entirely of ice. "The name's Cold Shoulder – *ice* to meet you. Your mum says you're going to *chill* with us here. . ."

"Oh, *do* stop with the ice puns, Cold Shoulder," sighed Madame Malice.

"GrOoW-ARRK-ssss!" boomed the third. He was a bizarre, monstrous mish mash of animal parts. One arm was a gorilla's, while the other was a python. His right leg was a kangaroo's, his left a tiger's. His massive head looked like a crocodile's with a lion's mane and on his back was a pair of eagle's wings.

"Creature Features is terribly loyal but he doesn't say much – unless you count the grunts and squawks," said Madame Malice. "Which is still more than you'll get from Gunk."

Tommy stared at the fourth figure – an inhuman blob of orange goo. It pulsated with artificial life. As Tommy peered, his own face formed in the goo and stared back at him.

"Gross. . ." said an impressed Tommy.

"Now, you're all to make my son feel at home," said Madame Malice. "He is my new second in command."

"Eh?" blurted Force Face. "But I thought I was—"

"Don't be silly, dear – you're not a *Malice*,"

105

replied Madame Malice. "So if Kid Malice needs anything – anything at all – he just needs to ask. Do I make myself clear?"

"Clear as ice."

"Got it."

"SQUAAWKuckoo!"

"In that case, it's official!" said Madame Malice with glee. "Kid Malice, welcome to your new life. Welcome to Chaos Incorporated!"

DOUBLE CROSS

THE ALBION ANALYSIS

MADAME MALICE'S NEW SIDEKICK?

**BOY WHO ATTACKED ALBION CITY
WEARING SUPERVILLAIN'S SKULL SYMBOL**

Tommy had been missing for two days. Captain Atomic abandoned his search for the remaining supervillains to look for his lost son. He had given strict instructions for the rest of the family to stay on the Island. For once, Jonny wanted to defy his father. He wanted to find his brother.

Then, after forty-eight long hours, Captain Atomic returned to the Island.

"Did you find him?" cried Jonny, appearing in a blur of super-speed as his father stepped out of the Atomic Bomber. "Where is he? Is he OK? Is he coming back?"

Captain Atomic bowed his head as Uncle Dogday and Aunt Sandwich emerged from the end of the corridor.

"I'm sorry, Jonny . . . I don't know where your brother is," said Captain Atomic, looking more exhausted than ever. "But I will find him, I promise."

"Let me help!" cried Jonny. "I'm as fast as you! I could cover the whole city in an hour!"

"Absolutely not," replied his father. "I want you here, where it's safe. I'm not about to risk losing you too."

"You said I had these powers to help people and you won't even let me help Tommy!" shouted Jonny.

"Jonny does have a point, Captain," said Uncle Dogday. "If you're not going to let him use his powers now, when they're needed most, then when?"

"And Jonny knows his brother better than anyone," said Aunt Sandwich. "I mean, it's not as if Tommy's just going to phone home, now is it?"

BRiiiiNG!

Everyone stared at the telephone on the wall. Then, in a blur of super-speed, Captain Atomic picked it up.

"Hello?" he said.

"Dad?" said a voice. "It's me. It's *Tommy*."

"Tommy!" cried Captain Atomic. "Are you all right? Where are you? No one's angry. I just want to know you're OK. . ."

"I'm fine, Dad," replied Tommy. "I'm great! Everything's great!"

"You are? It is?" asked Captain Atomic.

"Yeah, I'm having the *best* time!"

Tommy flew into the air, swooping around the great, dark cavern of Chaos Rock. "I've got this cool room and loads of toys and Mum's built me a swimming pool and I've got a bunch of new friends – Chaos Inc. are awesome! Cold Shoulder, Force Face and the rest – they're hardly evil at all when you get to know them. We just play all day and mess around with our powers."

"Where are you, Tommy?" asked Captain Atomic, bristling at the mention of his arch-enemies. "I need to know *where you are*."

"Don't worry. This is what I want!" said Tommy. He landed next to his mother, who waited in the shadows. "And it's Kid Malice now. How cool is that?"

"Kid . . . *Malice?*" repeated Captain Atomic.

"Mum said I should call and tell you. I'm her sidekick, you see," said Tommy, proudly. "Tell Jonny I've got a proper costume, with skulls and everything!"

"Tommy, put your mother on the phone," growled Captain Atomic.

Tommy held out the phone to Madame Malice, who plucked it gently from his hands. "Hello, Captain. Long time no battle."

"Malice!" he boomed. "Give me back my son or I'll—"

"Blah, blah, blah – still the same old Captain Blowhard," said Madame Malice with a mock yawn. "And before you start accusing me of bad parenting, let me remind you that Thomas came here of his own free will. My son is happy here, aren't you, my little raven?"

"Yeah!" said Tommy. "I'm Kid Malice!"

"Don't do this, Malice," said Captain Atomic.

"I'll do the talking, thank you very much," continued Madame Malice. "Listen carefully. Since you've failed to discover my secret lair in all these years, I'm going to keep this line open so you track it here. Come alone, unarmed and prepared to surrender. . . Or your son *dies*."

"Wait, what?" said Tommy.

"You have *four minutes*, my dear Captain," said Madame Malice before she flung the phone into the shadows.

SWEET SURRENDER

The Unlikely Albion
ATOMIC IN LEAGUE WITH VILLAINS PRISON BREAK A PUBLICITY STUNT TO BOOST CAPTAIN ATOMIC MERCHANDISE SALES, CLAIM EXPERTS

"It's about selling lunch boxes, not saving the world," says man in the street

"Uh, Mum?" began Tommy, a little confused. "What was that whole 'or your son dies' thing. . .?"

"All will become clear," said Madame Malice. Suddenly, Force Face appeared behind Tommy and clamped something around his neck. Tommy grasped at it and felt a cold metal disc encircling his neck like a collar. It locked shut and began to whirr.

"What's happening?" asked Tommy, suddenly feeling weak at the knees.

"That there's a power choker," grunted Force Face. "They use them to stop supervillains using their abilities. As long as you got that around your neck, you're just an ordinary kid."

"I didn't want to use you like this, my little raven," said Madame Malice. "But I am what I am! When I realized you were at school, out in the open, I knew I had discovered Captain Atomic's *greatest weakness*. I finally had a way to exact my revenge. All I had to do was get out of prison."

"So I got myself caught and sent to The Stronghold," said Force Face, proudly. "I built a secret EMP device into my face plate so I could shut down them power chokers. Bob's your uncle, we were *super* again."

"Freeing the other inmates ensured that your father was kept nice and busy," added Madame Malice. "I could take my time. . ."

"But what about – I mean, I'm your sidekick!" said Tommy, as the other members of Chaos Inc. emerged from the darkness.

"Oh, Thomas," chuckled Madame Malice. "It's been a delight having you here, but I really don't need a sidekick. What I need is *bait for a trap*. Speaking of which, here's your father now. . ."

BOOOOOM!

Captain Atomic crashed through the walls of Chaos Rock! His rocket pack lit up the darkness of Chaos Inc.'s secret base as he descended to the ground. Madame Malice grabbed Tommy in a psychic force field, holding him fast.

"Dramatic as ever! We do have a front door, you know," tutted Madame Malice. "Still, you're punctual, I'll give you that."

"Tommy! Are you all right?" said Captain Atomic.

"Y – yeah," said Tommy. "Sorry, Dad."

"Hush, dear – grown-ups are talking," said Madame Malice.

"Everything's going to be OK, son. Just remember, it's not your fault . . . it's your *mother's*," said Captain Atomic. He turned to Madame Malice.

"Now let my son go."

"All in good time," said Madame Malice. She drew a polished metal collar from her cloak and psychically floated it over to him. It hovered in front of Captain Atomic's face.

"You must recognize a power choker when you see one – you invented them, after all!" laughed Madame Malice. "Now, be a dear and put it around your neck."

Captain Atomic clenched his fists. "I need your word that if I do this, you'll let Tommy go."

"You have my word, Captain," said Madame Malice.

Tommy wiped a tear from his eye in time to see his father clamp the power choker around his neck. He immediately fell to his knees, powerless and weak.

"SUPER! OR RATHER, NOT,"

laughed Madame Malice, victoriously.

"Now ... let Tommy GO," growled Captain Atomic.

"Don't be silly," said Madame Malice. "Stick to my word? That wouldn't be very villainous, now would it? I am what I am! I am Madame Malice!"

THE RETURN OF
THE BLUE DYNAMO?

THE BABBLEBROOK BABBLE

BABBLEBROOK TEACHER HAS VERY BAD DAY

HOUSE AND SCHOOL DESTROYED UNDER

MYSTERIOUS CIRCUMSTANCES

Three hours had passed since Captain Atomic had jetted off to rescue Tommy. Jonny stared into space and wished he were anywhere – or any*one* – else in the world.

"Mum *knew* I'd tell Dad about the whole sidekick thing . . . she knew Tommy would feel like we were ganging up on him," said Jonny. "She tricked us all and now Dad's walking into a trap!"

"I – I'm sure everything will be fine," said Aunt Sandwich. "Your father is ever so resourceful. . ."

"What if it's not?" said Jonny. "I can't just sit here while Dad gets captured – or *worse*. I have to *do* something."

"Your father gave strict orders for us to wait here," said Uncle Dogday. "I'm afraid we'll just have to see what happens."

"What do you think is going to happen?" cried Jonny. "Mum's a supervillain, Dad's a superhero – they *hate* each other. That's the way it is – it's like cats and dogs!"

"Some of my best friends are cats," noted Uncle Dogday.

"I could have done something to stop this . . . and I didn't," said Jonny. He took his mask out of his pocket and crushed it in his hand. "I was having such a good time that I ignored what I knew, deep down – that my mum is a very, *very* bad person."

"Oh, Jonny. . ." squeaked Aunt Sandwich.

"Aunt Sandwich, Uncle Dogday – I know it's past my bedtime . . . but you have to let me try and save them."

Uncle Dogday and Aunt Sandwich looked at each other.

"Very well," said Uncle Dogday, finally. "But we're coming with you."

"Oh me, oh my – we're forming a super team!" squealed Aunt Sandwich. "Who else shall we call? We'll need an army of heroes to take on Chaos Inc. . ."

"I'm afraid no one's returning our calls," said Uncle Dogday. "Miss Mystery is fighting Ball 'n' Chain. The Unknown Quantity is tackling Smash

Man and his Smashtronauts. Mr V is battling Bounder and Cad. Power Punch and Judo Judy are, well, worse than *useless*. . ."

"So we're on our own?" said Aunt Sandwich, nervously. "Oh me, oh my. . ."

"There is one superhero who can help us," said Jonny. "I can't believe I'm saying this . . . but we need to go to Babblebrook."

Nineteen minutes later, Jonny, Uncle Dogday and Aunt Sandwich were hovering over Babblebrook village in an Atomic Bomber.

"Are you sure about this, Jonny?" asked Aunt Sandwich. "I thought you said Ms Crackdown *hates* superheroes. What makes you think she'll help us?"

"Ms Crackdown's horrible, but she *was* a superhero once," replied Jonny. "Anyway, she's got a score to settle. Mum smashed the school *and* her house."

"Then I think we might have found her – look down there!" yapped Uncle Dogday.

On an otherwise unremarkable lamp-lit street, one house stood out. It was squashed flat. In the driveway was a small electric-blue car.

"Let me do the talking," said Jonny as the Atomic Bomber landed silently next to the car. Jonny could just make out Ms Crackdown, asleep at the wheel. He took a deep breath and knocked on the window.

"You!" she snarled, hastily adjusting her wig as she wound down the window. "What are you doing here? Come to gloat?"

"Ms Crackdown—" began Jonny.

"Well, if you think I'm going to be scared off by petty vandalism then think again!" hissed Ms Crackdown.

"Ms Crackdown!"

"What?" hissed Ms Crackdown.

Jonny took another deep breath. "My mum is Madame Malice, the supervillain. She's got my brother – and I think she's going to try to kill my dad."

Ms Crackdown stared at Jonny for a long, tense moment.

"You'd better get in," she said.

Jonny, Uncle Dogday and Aunt Sandwich clambered on to the back seat of Ms Crackdown's car. One short explanation later and Ms Crackdown was up to speed on the Atomic family's predicament.

"That's quite a pickle," said Ms Crackdown. "But even if I was inclined to help, why come to me? Your father must have a *dozen* superheroes on his speed dial."

"Right now, we're all there is," replied Jonny.

"Twin A, I made a vow a long time ago that

I would never again become The Blue Dynamo, Defender of the Innocent. I'm not a superhero any more," said Ms Crackdown.

"But my mum is *evil*," said Jonny, desperately. "She humiliated you in front of the whole class. . . She squashed the school and your house!"

"I'm – I'm sorry," sighed Ms Crackdown. "That part of my life is over."

Jonny put his head into his hands. After a moment an idea flashed across his face.

"She's *remarkable*," he said.

"Remarkable?" repeated Ms Crackdown.

"Remarkable . . . extraordinary. . . She thinks she's better than you, better than me, better than anyone! And it's her whole *mission* in life to prove it!"

"Better. . ." snarled a bristling Ms Crackdown. She took a whistling breath through her nostrils and straightened her wig.

"Well, we can't have that, can we?" she added.

She opened the glove compartment and pulled out a neatly folded electric-blue costume. "I've kept it in here since I retired. Let's hope it still fits. . ."

PRISONERS AND PLANS

WHERE IS CAPTAIN ATOMIC?
Hero not answering calls for help
"HELP!" cry city's residents

Several hundred kilometres away, an Atomic Bomber zoomed invisibly through the night sky, carrying a decidedly odd bunch of would-be rescuers.

"I forgot how warm this costume is – I've got sweat patches on my sweat patches," grumbled Ms Crackdown. "So, what's the plan? I assume there *is* a plan and we're not just wandering blindly into the lair of a supervillain."

"Ummm. . ." murmured Jonny.

"You must *always* have a lesson plan," sighed Ms Crackdown. "I, for one, have always preferred the direct approach."

"*Ahem* – under the circumstances I would favour a more subtle strategy," interjected Uncle Dogday. "There's no way we can take on Chaos Inc. *and* hope to rescue the Captain and Tommy."

"Are we really going to base our plan on the advice of your pets, Twin A?" huffed Ms Crackdown. "What next? Shall we consult your goldfish?"

"Uncle Bubbles! May he rest in peace," said Aunt Sandwich. "Actually, I think you're *both* right. We need the element of surprise, enough time to find the prisoners . . . and a **SECRET WEAPON**."

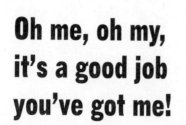

INTERLUDE
(AUNT SANDWICH'S SECRET WEAPON)

ALBION CITY SUN SAYS:

NO TIME FOR A HOLIDAY
"Lazy" Captain Atomic

hasn't saved anyone in days

"My cat's been stuck up a tree all night

and no sign of Captain Atomic. And I

only put the cat up there so I could meet

him," complains resident

Meanwhile, far underground within the depths of the volcano, Uncle Dogday and Aunt Sandwich had found their way inside Chaos Inc.'s secret base. They clambered down a winding air duct, the heat of the volcano's molten base already singeing their feet.

"The air ducts! Oh me, oh my, I never would have come up with this if it wasn't for Tommy's cunning. What a good boy!" chuckled Aunt Sandwich.

"We're getting close. The Captain's bio-signature is growing stronger," said Uncle Dogday, checking a small scanner attached to his right paw. "But I still don't feel right about leaving Jonny to deal with all those supervillains. . ."

"Jonny knows what he's doing. There's no way his mother will be able to resist putting him through his paces. And with them distracted, we can – WAIT!"

Aunt Sandwich peered through a vent in the air duct, the heat singeing her whiskers and burning her nose. There, far below, was Captain Atomic, dangling from his feet by a rope over a wide, deep pit filled with bubbling molten lava. She also spotted Tommy, tied up and helpless next to the pit, and Cold Shoulder, standing guard.

"OH ME, OH MY,

there they are!" whispered Aunt Sandwich.

"Lava pit *and* a super-powered guard. Madame Malice isn't taking any chances," noted Uncle Dogday, peering down through the vent.

"Then I suppose this would be a good time for a

SECRET WEAPON,"

whispered Aunt Sandwich. She reached into her cheek pouch and took out Captain Atomic's shrunken multi-gun.

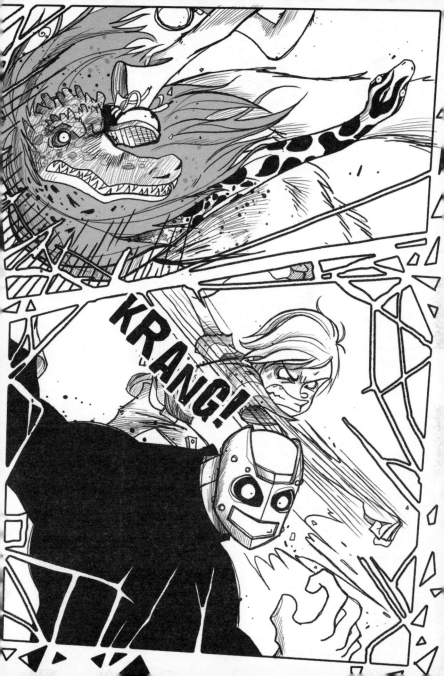

FLOMP!

HUH.

THAT wasn't so HARD...

Madame Malice floated in the air above Jonny as she pinned him to the ground with her force field.

"I didn't think you'd last ten seconds against my team!" said Madame Malice. "But you're still a *child*."

"Let . . . me . . . go!" grunted Jonny.

"You've been a bad boy – consider this the *naughty step*," said Madame Malice. "What did you think was going to happen? Did you think you could stop me single-handed?"

"Actually, he reported you to his teacher," said a voice. Madame Malice spun around to see a figure standing in the hole left by the Atomic Bomber.

"I know you . . . the tyrannical teacher! Oh, this is *priceless*!" Madame Malice guffawed. "Tommy has told me *all* about you, Ms Crackdown. Or should I be calling you *The Blue Dynamo* again? No, I know. . . Baldilocks from Babblebrook!"

With a psychic "flick" she threw off Ms

Crackdown's wig.

Ms Crackdown did not flinch.

"What are *you* going to do? Put me into *detention*?" chuckled Madame Malice. "Or dazzle me with your bald spot? Or make me laugh myself to death? Pray tell, what are you going to do?"

Ms Crackdown's breath whistled through her nostrils.

I'm going to teach you a **LESSON**, of course.

FREEING THE PRISONERS

THE SUPER SLEUTH
All Superheroes, All The Time

Is Ordinary the new Super?
Is our love affair with the superhero over?

It was Ms Crackdown's most powerful lightning bolt ever! Madame Malice crashed into a bank of machinery and fell to the ground, defeated.

"Jonny!" cried Ms Crackdown, prising Jonny from the ground. "Are you all right? Talk to me, Jonny!"

Jonny's eyes opened, just a crack.

"You . . . called me . . . Jonny," he wheezed.

Ms Crackdown raised an eyebrow. "Don't get used to it, Twin A."

"Fools. . . The heroes never win . . . in the end," said a voice. A smoking Madame Malice reached into a pocket in her cape and took out a skull-shaped communicator.

"Cold Shoulder . . . this is Madame Malice!" she cried. "Execute the plan! Execute Captain Atomic!"

"No!" whimpered Jonny.

There was a crackle on the communicator – then the sound of someone crying out.

"Dad . . . DAD!" cried Jonny.

"HA! I win! He is no more! Captain Atomic is dead!" shrieked Madame Malice.

"Dead? Oh me, oh my, no!" came the reply on the communicator.

KWOooOOM!

The ground burst open! Madame Malice scrambled for cover as plumes of smoke and ash rose up from the molten core of the volcano. She stared up in horror as four figures floated out of the smoke – a man, a boy, a dog and a hamster.

"It can't be – I'd won. . .!" whispered Madame Malice, as Tommy, free of his power choker, settled Captain Atomic, Uncle Dogday and Aunt Sandwich on what remained of the floor.

"Dad! Tommy!" cried Jonny, trying in vain to get up.

"Jonny!" shouted the Atomic family together. They gathered round and (carefully) gave him a hug.

"COLD SHOULDER! Where are you? You were supposed to be guarding the prisoners!" screamed Madame Malice into her communicator.

"Oh me, oh my! I almost forgot!" squeaked Aunt Sandwich. She reached into her cheek pouch again and took out a penny-sized, petrified Cold Shoulder! He was not quite a centimetre tall. "My mini multi-gun gave me the idea to shrink him. Just one of its fifty-seven settings!"

Tommy used his powers to lift Jonny to his feet,

but he could barely look his brother in the eye.

"Jonny . . . you were right," he said. "Mum's not a nice person. I mean, *at all*."

"Tell me about it," replied Jonny, holding his ribs.

"Now, what do you say to your brother, Tommy?" said Captain Atomic, sternly.

Tommy sighed and kicked the dust at his feet.

"Sorry for putting you and the family and the whole world in terrible danger," he muttered.

"Good boy. Now let's clean up the rest of this—" began Captain Atomic, looking around at the supervillains strewn about the place. "Jonny – did you defeat the *whole* of Chaos Inc. all by yourself?"

"I had a bit of help," grunted Jonny. He pointed to Ms Crackdown as she replaced her wig on her head.

"Captain Atomic, allow me to introduce The Blue Dynamo," said Uncle Dogday. "The final member or our little rescue team."

"The Blue Dynamo?" repeated Captain Atomic. "I remember you from years ago! What happened? Why did you—"

"I'm not one for pleasantries, Captain Fancy-Pants," replied Ms Crackdown. "Let's just say I'm reasonably glad you're not dead and leave it at that."

"Foolish . . . fools!" wailed Madame Malice, dragging herself to her feet and raising her arms. "You really think you've *won*? You really think I wouldn't have a contingency plan? Witness the true power of Madame Malice – the power to make this volcano *erupt*, taking each and every one of you with it!"

The ground began to shake and boiling lava spewed out of the hole in the floor. Everyone braced themselves and looked for an escape route. . .

Everyone except Tommy.

He calmly looked down at his hand. In it was a power choker.

"I'm sorry, Mum," he said. "But I've decided I want to live with Dad. I am what I am, too . . . I'm an *Atomic*."

He released his grip, propelling the power choker across the room with his mind. Within a split second, it hooked around Madame Malice's neck – and clamped shut.

CHUNG!

"What? No – no! Not again! Ungrateful child, get this off me!" screamed Madame Malice, the power choker locked tightly around her neck. She clawed at the collar, wildly, her powers suddenly lost to her. "Get it OFF! I won't go back to being ordinary! I WON'T! I'm MADAME MALICE!"

Tommy and Jonny stared at their mother as she raged.

"Mum," said Tommy, softly, "you *really* need to go back to prison."

INTERESTING TIMES

Albion City Telegraph

"NEARLY THERE"

Captain Atomic promises to recapture the last of the escaped supervillains – and proves it by nabbing the whole of Chaos Inc. "I had a little help – actually, a lot of help," admits Atomic

By morning, Captain Atomic had already arranged to repair the damage caused by Madame Malice's reign of terror – and by his own son.

"All that's going to take a *long* time to pay off from your pocket money," smirked Jonny, as

Uncle Dogday and Aunt Sandwich tended to the boys' wounds. "Maybe you should get a paper round. . ."

"Shut up, *Jonny*," grumbled Tommy. "I don't see you complaining that we don't have to go to school tomorrow."

"Actually, I wanted to talk to you about that," said Captain Atomic, striding into the room. "I was wondering how you might feel about *not* going back to school. At least, not for the moment."

"So we just go back to being taught at home?" groaned Tommy. "That's even *worse* – Uncle Dogday's lessons are always about dogs! No offence, Uncle Dogday."

"Humph!" snorted Uncle Dogday.

"What do you care, Tommy? You're *grounded* for ever, remember?" said Jonny, slapping his brother on the arm.

Captain Atomic took a deep breath and folded his arms.

"We live in interesting times, boys. I'm not excusing what *either* of you did. You were wrong to lie to me about your mother. And Tommy, you *are* going to make up for the damage you caused and the lives you affected. You have to learn to be responsible with your power."

"I know, but—" began Tommy.

"*But*," continued their dad, "I see now that a lot of what's happened is my fault. I've spent so long trying to keep you safe, I ended up putting you in danger. I'm starting to wonder whether you'd be safer . . . happier . . . *out in the open.*"

"Out in the open?" repeated Jonny and Tommy, together.

"I was wondering how you might feel about being introduced to the world," said Captain Atomic. "I was wondering if you'd like to become my *sidekicks*."

"No way!" squealed Tommy. "And you promise you won't use me as bait for your arch-enemy?"

"I promise," chuckled Captain Atomic. He turned to Jonny. "No pressure, son. You don't have to be anything you don't want to be."

"I—" began Jonny, not sure what to say. He thought back over the strangest week of his life – and to that night, fighting for his life against Chaos Inc. and his own mother. A smile spread across his face.

"Bring it on,"

he said.

"Oh me, oh my! How exciting!" squealed Aunt
Sandwich.

For the first time in weeks, laughter rang out

across Atomic Island. The future was suddenly a wide-open book, but one thing appeared certain:

Jonny and Tommy were going to be

SUPERHEROES.

LOOK OUT FOR MORE

ATOMIC!

ADVENTURES

Photo credit: Catherine Shakespeare Lane

Guy Bass grew up dreaming of being a
superhero – he even had a Spider-Man costume.
The costume doesn't fit any more, so Guy
now contents himself with writing books and
plays. His previous books include MONSTER
MADNESS, MONSTER MAYHEM, ALIEN
INVASION and ALIEN ESCAPE. Guy lives in
London with his wife and no dog, yet.

www.guybass.com

ASK GUY BASS

1. Did you ever want to be a superhero when you were younger?

That was all I wanted to be. . . Superman, Tarzan, The Hulk, Spider-Man – they were my heroes growing up. As soon as I could walk I wished I could fly. As soon as I could write and draw I was making up my own superheroes. I think deep down I thought I was definitely going to end up as an actual superhero. Imagine my disappointment!

2. If you could have any super power, what would it be and why?

I always wanted to fly but I'm not a fan of heights so I'd probably never get too high off the ground. I'd look like a panicked chicken . . . in a cape. Or I might go for one of the more obscure powers, just to be different – invisible legs, memory-loss sneezes, the ability to turn into a shoe. . .

3. What would your superhero name be?

I'd like a cool name like Marvellous Man or Captain Cobra, but I'm pretty sure all the good names are taken. I'd probably end up as Power Pigeon or Haircut Man or The Blazing Toilet.

4. Apart from ones featuring superheroes, what were your favourite books growing up?

George's Marvellous Medicine by Roald Dahl, the Hal and Roger *Adventure* books by Willard Price, the *Silver Brumby* series, and an amazing little book called *Dinosaurs*, which was all about dinosaurs.

5. Do you have any tips for budding superheroes?

Don't try to fly before you can walk.

6. Are you actually a secret superhero?

If occasionally wearing your underwear on the outside of your clothes makes you a superhero, then yes!

LOOK OUT FOR MORE FROM GUY BASS

LOOK OUT FOR MORE FROM
GUY BASS

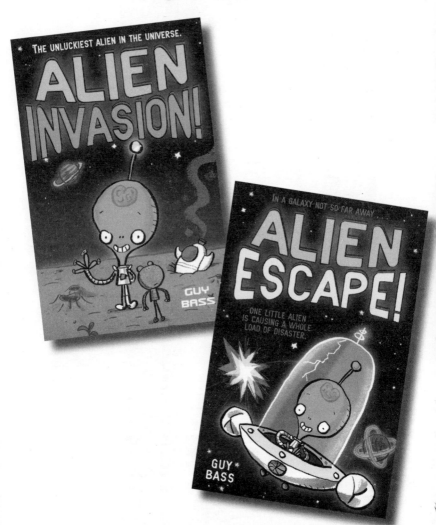